A Day at the Beach

Ed Briant

Greenwillow Books
An Imprint of HarperCollinsPublishers

To create the full-color art, the artist constructed figures using clay and wire,
and built sets using cardboard, wire, and glue. The figures and sets were painted
with acrylic paint and digitally photographed. The digital photos were then
composited together on a laptop computer using a drawing tablet.
The text type is 26-point Bernhard Gothic Heavy.

Library of Congress Cataloging-in-Publication Data
Briant, Ed.
A day at the beach / by Ed Briant.
   p. cm.
"Greenwillow Books."
Summary: When they arrive at the beach, two young pandas discover
throughout the day that they need their swimsuits, goggles, and shovels,
until the driving back and forth to retrieve the items makes their father
come up with a creative idea.
ISBN-10: 0-06-079981-1 (trade bdg.) ISBN-13: 978-0-06-079981-6 (trade bdg.)
ISBN-10: 0-06-079982-X (lib. bdg.) ISBN-13: 978-0-06-079982-3 (lib. bdg.)
[1. Beaches—Fiction. 2. Pandas—Fiction. 3. Fathers—Fiction.] I. Title.
PZ7.B75883Day 2006 [E]—dc22 2005022176

First Edition 10 9 8 7 6 5 4 3 2 1

Greenwillow Books

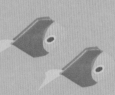

For the sixteen hundred giant pandas who remain
in the bamboo forests of western China,
and for the people who look after them.

One perfect morning, Dad drove Alice B. and Baxter to look at the ocean.

It was clear and blue,
with tiny waves that sparkled in the sun.

"The water looks so nice," said Baxter.
"I wish we had our swimsuits."
"Let's go back and get them," said Alice B.
"It'll only take half an hour."

Dad drove Baxter and Alice B.
back to the house.

They changed   into their swimsuits,

and Dad took them back to the beach.

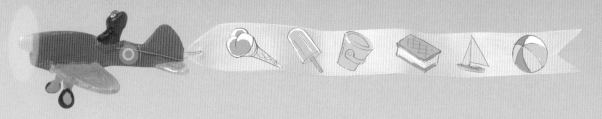

Alice B. and Baxter ran straight to the ocean and dived in.

The water felt really good.

"Wow, look at all those fish," said Baxter.
"I wish we had our goggles."
"Let's go back and get them," said Alice B.
"It'll only take half an hour."

Dad drove Baxter and Alice B.
back to the house.

They found their goggles,

and Dad took them back to the beach.

Baxter and Alice B. swam underwater
and looked at all the fish.

After that, they played on the sand.
Alice B. did a cartwheel.

"I wish I had my camera," said Baxter.
"Let's go back and get it," said Alice B.
"It'll only take half an hour."

Dad drove Baxter and Alice B.
back to the house.

They found Baxter's camera,

and Dad took them back to the beach.

Baxter took some pretty pictures of Alice B.

Alice B. took some silly ones of Baxter.

"Hey, Baxter," said Alice B.

"I bet I could make a better sand castle than you."

"I wish we had our shovels," said Baxter.

"Let's go back and get them," said Alice B.

"It'll only take half an hour."

Dad drove Baxter and Alice B.
back to the house.

They found their shovels.

But this time . . .

Dad drove them back to the beach in his big truck.
In the back were the shovels and absolutely everything else
that Dad could think of.

It was very hard to say whose castle was the best.

"It's hot," said Alice B.

"I wish Bucky Henderson was here," said Baxter.

"We could use his paddleboat."

"Let's go back and get him," said Alice B.

"It'll only take half an hour."

"Who needs a paddleboat when you've got me?" asked Dad, lifting Baxter and Alice B. high up in the air.

Dad took off his shirt.

Then he charged down the beach
and jumped into a wave with a big . . .

Splish.

Dad floated on his back while
Baxter and Alice B. sat on his tummy.

They watched the sailboats flying over the waves.

On the way home, they stopped for ice cream.

It only took them half an hour.